Flip through the pages to see Iggy dance!

This Book Belongs To

. . . .

Text copyright © 1998 Vivian French
Illustrations copyright © 1998 David Melling

This edition first published 1998
by Hodder Children's Books

The right of Vivian French and David Melling to be identified
as the Author and Illustrator of the Work has been asserted by
them in accordance with the Copyright, Designs and Patents
Act 1988.

10   9   8   7

A Catalogue record for this book is available from the British
Library

ISBN 0340 71360 7

Printed and bound in Great Britain by
Omnia Books Limited, Glasgow

Hodder Children's Books
A Division of Hodder Headline Limited
338 Euston Road
London NW1 3BH

Iggy Pig's Skippy Day

Vivian French

Illustrated by David Melling

Hodder
Children's
Books

a division of Hodder Headline Limited

For David M.
with many thanks
Love Viv

For Daniel Hall
D.M.

Iggy Pig was skipping.

"Watch me skip, Mother Pig!
Watch me skip!"

"OINK!" said Mother Pig.
"I'm watching, my own
dear little pig. Now don't
go skipping too far!"

Iggy Pig went skipping
around the farmyard.

"Skip skip skip
I can skip all day
Over the hills and far away!"
he sang.

On top of the
haystack was
a big grey animal.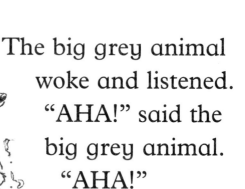

The big grey animal
woke and listened.
"AHA!" said the
big grey animal.
"AHA!"

The big grey
animal slid off
the haystack.
"Cooee, Iggy
Pig, Cooee!"

Iggy Pig never stopped
skipping.
"Who are you?" he asked.

"Just a friend," said the big
grey animal. "Iggy Pig, Iggy
Pig - may I skip with you?"

"Yes, yes!" said Iggy Pig.
"Do come and skip with me!"
Iggy Pig went skipping
through the gate.

The big grey animal
skipped behind him.

"Skip skip skip
We can skip all day
Over the hills and far away!"
sang Iggy Pig.

"Cluck! Cluck! Iggy Pig!"
clucked Chicky Chick.
"May I skip with you?"

"Yes, yes, Chicky Chick!" said
Iggy Pig. "Do come and skip
with us!"

Iggy Pig went skipping down
the lane.

The big grey animal skipped
behind him.

Chicky Chick skipped behind
the big grey animal.

"Skip skip skip
We can skip all day
Over the hills and far away!"
sang Iggy Pig.

"Baa! Baa! Iggy Pig!"
called Lucky Lamb.
"May I skip with you?"

"Yes, yes, Lucky Lamb!"
said Iggy Pig. "Do come
and skip with us!"

Iggy Pig went skipping across the field.

The big grey animal skipped behind him.

Chicky Chick skipped behind the big grey animal.

Lucky Lamb skipped behind Chicky Chick.

"Skip skip skip
We can skip all day
Over the hills and far away!"
sang Iggy Pig.

Bunny Rabbit was under
the trees.
She saw Iggy Pig skipping
across the field.

"Iggy Pig! Iggy Pig!
Where are you going?"
"Hullo, Bunny Rabbit!"
said Iggy Pig. "Come and
skip with us."

Iggy Pig went skipping up
the hill.

The big grey animal skipped
behind him.

Chicky Chick skipped behind
the big grey animal.

Lucky Lamb skipped behind
Chicky Chick.

Bunny Rabbit skipped behind
Lucky Lamb.

"Skip skip skip
We can skip all day
Over the hills and far away!"
sang Iggy Pig.

At the top of the hill Iggy Pig
skipped in a circle.
The big grey animal skipped
behind him.

"Cluck! Cluck!" clucked
Chicky Chick.
"Iggy Pig, I have skipped
too far! I want to go home
to my farmyard!"

"Baa! Baa!" said Lucky Lamb.
"I want to go home to my
field!"

"That's right!" said Bunny
Rabbit. "It's time to go home,
Iggy Pig!"

Iggy Pig did not stop skipping.

"No no!" he said,
"I can skip all day
Over the hills and far away!"

"That's right, Iggy Pig,"
said the big grey animal.
"And I will skip with you
wherever you go!"

Iggy Pig went skipping over the hill.
The big grey animal skipped behind him.

"Skip skip skip
We can skip all day
Over the hills and far away!"
sang Iggy Pig.

Bunny Rabbit, Lucky Lamb
and Chicky Chick went home.

Dusty Dog was running
around the farmyard.

"Where have you been, Chicky
Chick?" he asked.
"I've been skipping," said
Chicky Chick. "I've been
skipping with Iggy Pig."

"And where is Iggy Pig now?"
asked Dusty Dog.
"Over the hills and far away,"
said Chicky Chick.

"I see," said Dusty Dog. "And
is he on his own?"
"Oh NO," said Chicky Chick.
"There's a big grey animal
skipping just behind him."

"WOOF!" said Dusty Dog.
"WOOF WOOF WOOF!"

Dusty Dog dashed out of the
farmyard.

"Cluck! Cluck!" clucked Chicky Chick. "Dusty Dog has gone to skip with Iggy Pig!"

Iggy Pig was still skipping.
The big grey animal skipped
behind him.

"Iggy Pig, Iggy Pig," said the
big grey animal.
"Shall we stop for a rest?"

"No, no!" said Iggy Pig,
and he skipped faster.

The big grey animal began
to puff.

Iggy Pig went skipping
down the hill.
The big grey animal puffed
behind him.

"Iggy Pig, Iggy Pig," puffed
the big grey animal. "I think
we should stop for a rest.
I think we should stop for
a drink."

"No, NO!" said Iggy Pig, and
he skipped faster than ever.

The big grey animal began
to pant.

Iggy Pig went skipping
around the hill.
The big grey animal puffed
and panted behind him.

"Iggy Pig! Iggy Pig!
It's time to stop!
Iggy Pig! Iggy Pig!
I'm hungry!"

"No, no!" said Iggy Pig, and
he skipped higher and higher.

The big grey animal began
to limp.

Iggy Pig skipped back
across the field.
The big grey animal puffed
and panted and limped
behind him.

"Stop, Iggy Pig! Stop!"
he panted.

"No, no!" said Iggy Pig as he skipped round and round.

"Iggy Pig," growled the big grey animal. "If you don't stop skipping AT ONCE I shall eat you ALL UP!"

"Oh no," said Iggy Pig.
"You'll have to catch me first."
And Iggy Pig went skipping
down the lane.

The big grey animal stopped.
"I just can't skip another skip,"
he moaned.

The big grey animal sat down
JUST as Dusty Dog dashed up.
"OH! OH! OH!" moaned the
big grey animal.

"WOOF!" barked Dusty Dog,
and he chased the big grey
animal. "WOOF! WOOF!"

He chased him across
the field and over the hill.

He chased him over the hills
and far away.

Iggy Pig skipped all the way
home to the farmyard.
"Skip skip skip
I skipped all day
Over the hills and far away!"
sang Iggy Pig.

"Did you skip *all* day, my dear
Iggy Pig?" asked Mother Pig.

"Yes," said Iggy Pig.
"Bunny Rabbit, Lucky Lamb
and Chicky Chick couldn't
skip like me.
Even the big grey animal
couldn't skip like me."

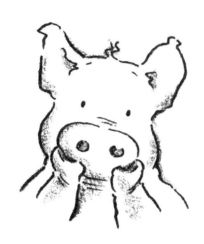

"OINK!" said Mother Pig.
"OINK! OINK! OINK!
Iggy Pig! Iggy Pig! Have you
been skipping with a WOLF?"

Iggy Pig didn't answer.
Iggy Pig was fast asleep.